Round the Turkey
A Grateful Thanksgiving

written by Leslie Kimmelman

illustrated by Nancy Cote

www.av2books.com

Published by AV² by Weigl
350 5ᵗʰ Avenue, 59ᵗʰ Floor New York, NY 10118
Copyright ©2013 AV² by Weigl

Printed in the United States of America in North Mankato, Minnesota
1 2 3 4 5 6 7 8 9 0 16 15 14 13 12

052012
WEP160512

Library of Congress Cataloging-in-Publication Data

Kimmelman, Leslie.
Round the turkey : a grateful Thanksgiving / written by Leslie Kimmelman ; illustrated by Nancy Cote.
  p. cm.
Summary: As they gather to celebrate Thanksgiving Day, members of an extended family take turns describing, in
rhyme, the things that make them feel grateful.
ISBN 978-1-61913-130-9 (hardcover : alk. paper)
[1. Stories in rhyme. 2. Thanksgiving Day--Fiction. 3. Family life--Fiction.] I. Cote, Nancy, ill. II Title.
PZ8.3.K5598Ro 2012
[E]--dc23
                                                 2012021689

Go to **www.av2books.com**, and enter this book's unique code.

BOOK CODE

L630952

AV² by Weigl brings you media enhanced books that support active learning.

Follow these steps to access your AV² book.

Step 1
Use the book code above.

Step 2
Enter the code at www.av2books.com.

Step 3
Explore your Fiction readalong.

Uncle Dave

Milo

Peggy

Mom

Jonah

Dad

Kaitlyn

Aunt Terry

Jesse

Ike

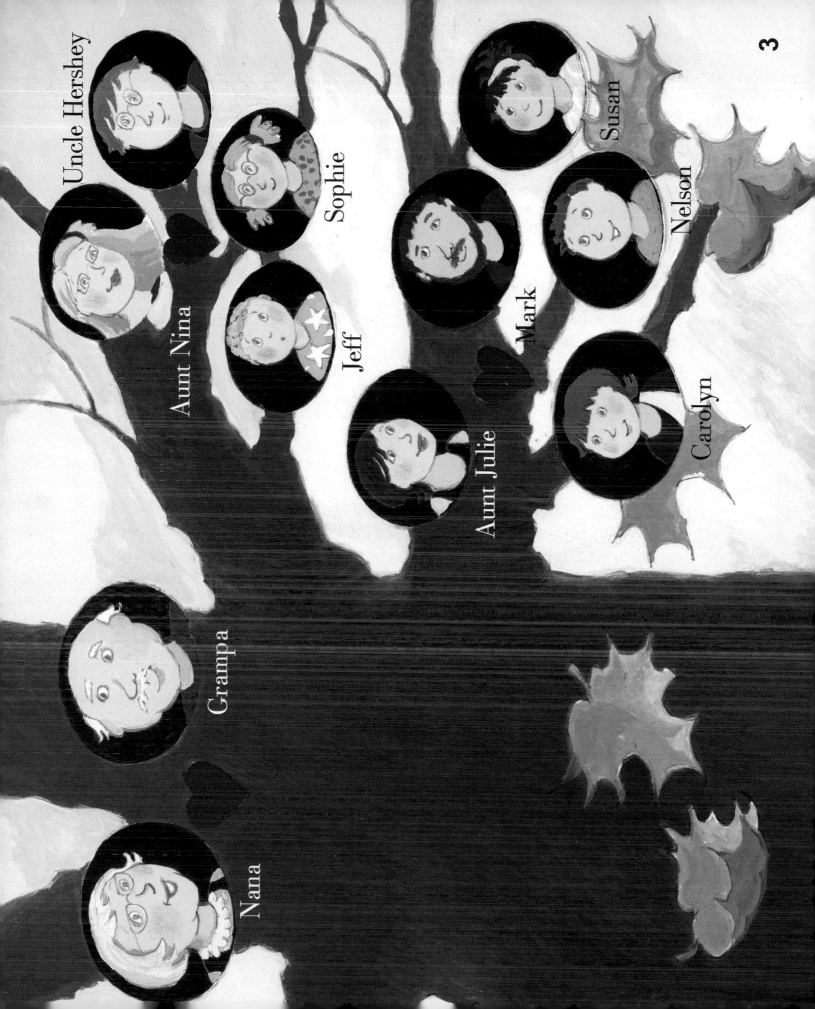

My Turn (Jesse)

They're coming from near
and they're coming from far,
by plane and by train
and by bike and by car.
They can't wait to be
where the others all are—
everyone's coming to my house.

They're coming for turkey
and stuffing and pie,
for hugs and for kisses
and handshakes and "hi,"
for talking and laughing
till midnight goodbye—
my family, together, at my house!

Nana's Turn

It's Thanksgiving,
it's November.
Take a minute
to remember
all the blessings
of the year,
round the table,
starting here.

Aunt Terry's Turn

Our family had three:
it was Milo, Dave, and me.
We had love to spare,
so decided to share.

Now far away, waiting,
was our little Kaitlyn.
We flew through the night
and gathered her tight.

Mother
母

Father
父

Family
家

Brother
弟

Uncle Dave's Turn

Today we are four,
and who could want more?

Kaitlyn's Turn

I like
my dog, Ike.

Ike's Turn

Woof woof
woof woof woof
woof woof drool
GRR
woof woof woof
slurp.

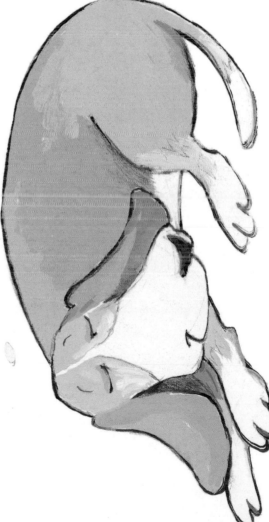

Psst. Want some turkey, Ike?

Milo's Turn

We had a school assembly
and everybody came:
the principal, the teachers,
and Mayor What's-His-Name.

We said the pledge of allegiance,
but that's not the whole story.
When it was time to sing some
songs, I got to hold Old Glory.

I didn't slouch or dip the flag,
I stood up straight and proud—
right through "God Bless America,"
the music growing loud.

We sang of purple majesties
and amber waves of grain.
We sang so loud they heard us
down on Fifty-first and Main.

Now others shared the stage with me, and some made speeches, too. But I'm the guy who held up high the great red, white, and blue.

Carolyn's Turn

I climbed a tree
to save a cat.
My pants got torn.
I lost my hat.

I grabbed the cat
without a fight.
I slithered down
and held it tight.

And then, kaboom!
I slipped and fell.
I hit the ground
and gave a yell.

The ambulance
was really cool.
I got to miss
two days of school!

Can I sign your cast, Carolyn?
Sure, Jesse.

Nelson's Turn

Tina, Deena, Max, and Mike, George the Third, Bernard, and Spike, Woody, Wendell, Wanda Lee, Genghis Khan and Dapper D., Molly, Lolly, Malcolm, Jim, Gabe and Babe and Fats and Slim— in my tanks, swim and swish, lots of thanks for all my fish.

Hey, Nelson, we got you a new one for Thanksgiving. His name is Pumpkin Pie.

Cool! Thanks, Jesse.

Thuthan'th (Susan's) Turn

Every Thaturday, all latht year,
I went to thee Mith V andermeer.

My thpeaking thkillth were quite a meth;
Mith V. helped me with letter "eth."

I practithed hard, and finally,
"You've got it now!" Mith V. told me.

I feel tho proud, tho thatithfied,
I knew I'd get it if I tried.

"I think you need more work," you thay?
I lotht two teeth thith Thaturday.

Way to go, Susan!

Mark and Julie's Turn

Late for work.
Missed the train.
Hole in sock.
Caught in rain.
Coughed and sneezed.
Throat felt sore.
Lost my watch.
How much more?
Spilled my soup.
Spilled my tea.
I looked up.
You saw me.

THANKS!

Is Aunt Julie getting married
again, Mom?
She sure is, Jesse.

Sophie's Turn

This is my brother, Jeffrey.
I'm thankful that he's here.
He's only been my brother
for one month and a year.
He learned his first word yesterday.
He's gonna say it now.
Okay, Jeffie, it's your turn.
Say the word, Jeff:

WOW.

He drools a bit; he sleeps too much—
but Jeffie, take a bow.
You'll just keep getting better.
The word for that is . . .

WOW!

Uncle Hershey's Turn

Just a minute. I'm still chewing.
Okay, ready now.

Turkey with stuffing,
cranberry muffin,
ripe red tomatoes,
yams and potatoes,
succotash,
yellow squash,
beets,
sweets,
pumpkin pie,
my, oh, my.
Rub-a-dub-dub—
thanks for the grub!

Hey, Jesse, pass the gravy, will you?

Aunt Nina's Turn

Look, everyone—it's snowing!

Falling, dancing, soft-lace flakes
blanketing the world with white.
What could be as magical
as snowfall on Thanksgiving night?
Outside: hushed, enchanted land.
Inside: noisy, loving clan.
Falling, dancing, soft-lace flakes
blanketing the world with white.
First snow of the winter season—
thanks for such an awesome sight.

Peggy's Turn

Hiya, Zack.
Yeah, it's me.
Yakity-yak.
I agree.
Eight o'clock?
Yakity-yak.
I'll ask Jill.
Call me back.

Yo, it's me.
Yakity-yak.
Got a dress.
Pink and black.
Eight o'clock.
Meet out back.
See you then.
Yakity-yak.

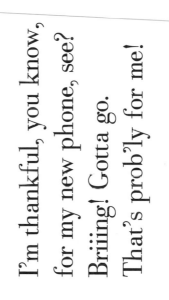

I'm thankful, you know,
for my new phone, see?
Briiing! Gotta go.
That's prob'ly for me!

Abby! Hey!
How was track?
Second place!
Yakity-yak.
Pretty mad.
Blew her stack.
Catch you later.
Yakity-yak.

Mom and Dad's Turn

Thanks for Peggy,
Jonah, Jesse—
sometimes loud
and sometimes messy;
sometimes pick
a silly fight;
sometimes up
too late at night;
rarely listen
when we call;
often drive us
up the wall.
But worry though we may about them,
watch our hair grow gray about them,
still, we'd like to say about them;
wouldn't want one day without them!

Jonah's Turn

Ninth inning,
loaded bases.
Two men out,
anxious faces.
Sweaty hands,
steady bat.

OUT
OF
THE
BALLPARK!
Thanks for that.

Grampa's Turn

Roof is holding.
Car still runs.
Got some hair left;
having fun.

Heart's a-beating,
hear just fine.
Lots of grandkids
to call mine.

So please pass me another plateful.
For this year, I'm truly grateful.

I love you, Grampa.
I love you too, Jesse.

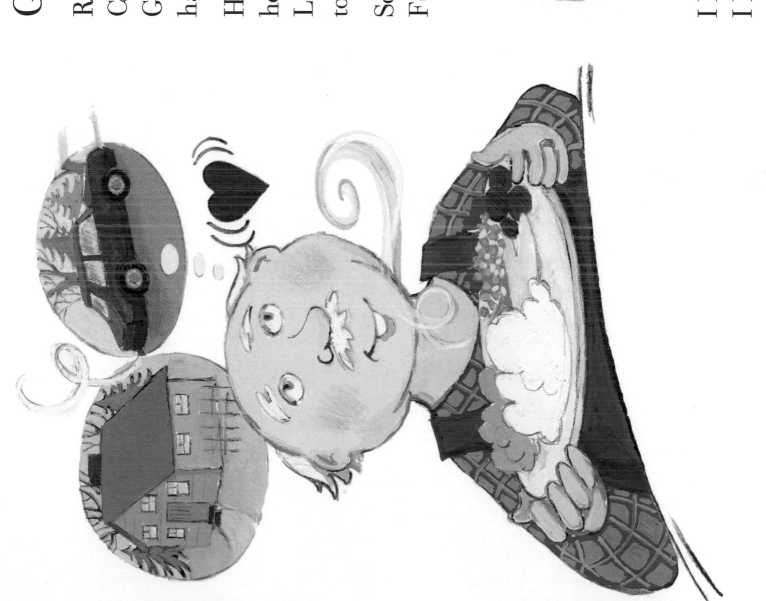

My Turn (again)

This has been the best Thanksgiving ever.

Going home 'neath shining moon;
thank you, thank you—come back soon!